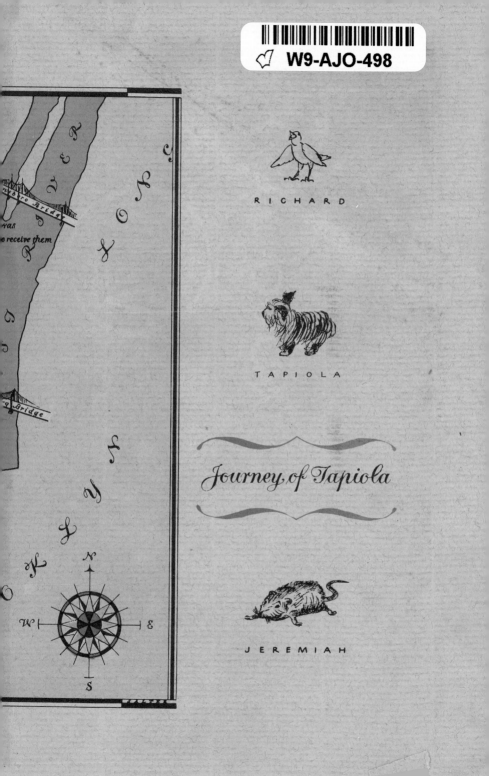

RICHARD

TAPIOLA

Journey of Tapiola

JEREMIAH

Hilda McAdams

Christmas 1938

Journey of Tapiola

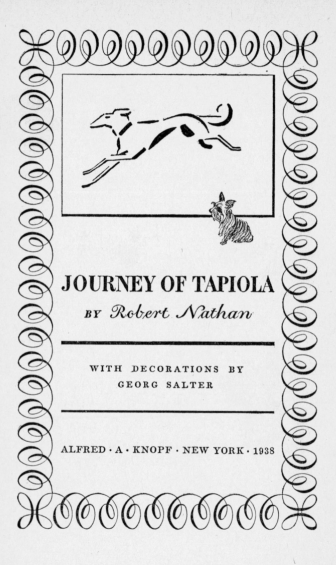

JOURNEY OF TAPIOLA

BY *Robert Nathan*

WITH DECORATIONS BY
GEORG SALTER

ALFRED · A · KNOPF · NEW YORK · 1938

To Miss Lucie-Lee, ma'am

Journey of Tapiola

~~~~~~~~~~~~~~~~~~~~~

Journey of Tapiola

TAPIOLA was a York-
shire terrier. His body, which was about
twelve inches long, and felt to the touch like
a squab or a young bird, was covered with
blue and silver hair; and he usually wore a
little ribbon on top of his head. His eyes held
a mournful and mysterious expression, de-

spite the ribbon which gave him a drunken appearance.

Tapiola belonged to Mrs. Poppel, the wife of the publisher; and so he was well acquainted with the literary scene. More than once he had reason to observe that success is not so much the result of muscular force as of self esteem.

But on one occasion he heard the eminent critic, Mr. Stuart Orrin, remark,

"We have returned to the age of heroes; and we admire today only the man who is without pity or other sentimental considerations of that sort."

Recognizing himself in this description, Tapiola experienced a feeling of pride, and determined to be worthy of Mrs. Poppel insofar as possible. For this reason, meeting the

Great Dane, Ch. Lance von Habich, on Fifth Avenue, he said to him,

"It is only your great size which makes you in any way remarkable."

Ch. Lance von Habich did not reply, for he considered Tapiola beneath his notice.

Tapiola then considered giving Ch. Lance von Habich a good bite on the leg, but thought better of it, and went away and hid behind Mrs. Poppel.

He was unhappy because he realized that Yorkshire terriers were not popular, due to the fact that they were small and did not seem quite real except to their owners. On the other hand, he liked to say of large dogs that they were only good for herding sheep, or hunting wolves. He was proud of his wits; and often said that to be so small and to live so well was after all something of an accomplishment.

All the same, he secretly admired the wolf-hounds and the airedales, whom everybody liked to pat on the head. He wished to be loved; and to have sharp teeth which people would respect.

One day he heard his mistress say to her husband, the publisher, Alfred Poppel,

"It is almost impossible to have a popular success these days under a thousand pages."

Tapiola had one great fault, which was that he always imagined that everybody was talking about him. Now he thought that Mrs. Poppel was talking about him, too. Putting his tail as far between his legs as he could, he retired with a crestfallen air to a dark place behind the sofa, and sat down to think things

over. It is true, he thought, that I am too
small; and the ribbon in my hair does not
make me look any bigger. And now even
Mrs. Poppel admits that I cannot have a
great popular success. Why is this? The
reason is that little dogs like me have never
caught the public fancy. What we need is a
hero for everyone to admire. Suppose I were
to kill a number of wolves which were about
to eat Mrs. Poppel?

And he grew hot with fright and exulta-
tion at this thought.

"That's it," he exclaimed. "I should be
very popular then."

At this moment a moth, disturbed from its
nap, flew past Tapiola's head like a bat or a
demon. The little terrier closed his eyes in
terror, and prepared for death. After a while

he opened them again, and smiled feebly at the sofa leg. Well, he thought, with a wolf it would at least be in the open.

And he reflected how much of his life was spent in such places as behind the sofa, where it was impossible to accomplish anything of an heroic nature. It is clear, he thought, that if I am going to provide the world with a hero, I shall have to leave Mrs. Poppel, and go out into the world where it is possible to find something heroic to do. Only, Mrs. Poppel will never allow it.

And he gazed gloomily at the sofa leg, to which he seemed bound by invisible bands.

Nevertheless, it was not long after this that an opportunity arose for him to leave Mrs. Poppel's house without being seen. Tapiola said goodbye to his possessions which con-

sisted of a rubber ball, a bone also made of
rubber, and a wicker basket with a silk pillow
and an eiderdown quilt. "Goodbye," he said
to them, "treasures of my youth, and little
basket in which I have spent so many comfortable nights. I am going where there will
not be any silk pillows or eiderdown quilts;
but when I return, it will be as someone who
has accomplished something in this world."

So saying, he disappeared out of the door,
and around the corner of the service stair-
way.

On his way to the street, he stopped at the third floor to say goodbye to his friend the canary who lived in a cage in Mrs. Sweeney's kitchen. When Dicky heard that Tapiola was going out to be a hero, he became very thoughtful and dejected. Presently he remarked,

"Tapiola, I am in the same fix as you. To call a singer a canary these days is to express nothing but disdain. I should like to show people that I, too, can be manly, even though I have not got the deep chest tones of Nelson Eddy, or Mr. Tibbett."

Tapiola replied, "I am sure that you would have a great success, if only enough people could hear you."

"Do you really think so?" asked Dicky anxiously.

"I am sure of it."

"Then I will go with you," exclaimed the canary. "We will be heroes together."

Tapiola was delighted to have his friend for company, as he had been afraid that he might be a little lonesome. So he was more than willing to wait while the canary opened with his beak the door of his cage, and took a last peck at the piece of apple which hung between the bars. "I do not know when I will have an apple again," he said, "but I am ready to sacrifice everything for my art.

"One thing, however, I must insist on," he added, as he fluttered to the ground in front of Tapiola's nose: "I do not want to be known as Dicky any more. Hereafter please call me Richard."

Tapiola agreed to do so, and the two

friends proceeded down the back stairs to the service entrance. There they hid, not without misgivings, in an empty ash can which some-one had turned over on its side. "It would be very distressing," said Tapiola, "if Mrs. Pop-pel came by at this point. Let us wait here until it grows dark, and then no one will see us as we leave."

But Richard did not like the idea of wait-ing in an ash can. "Would it not be better," he suggested, "to fly away now, while the pigeons are still wheeling in the skies?" Tapi-ola reminded his friend that he could not fly. "That is too bad," said Richard, who had not thought about it before. "In that case, I do not see how we will ever get anywhere at all."

"Never mind," said Tapiola; "we must trust somewhat to fate."

At that moment the ash can was seized by a street cleaner, lifted high in the air, and emptied into a truck belonging to the Department of Sanitation and Garbage Removal. Tapiola and Richard found themselves among a lot of old bottles, and smothered in ashes. "Are you hurt, Richard?" cried Tapiola when he had got his breath.

"No," said Richard; "I am surprised, that is all." And he set to work to preen and ruffle his feathers which gave off a shower of dust.

Seeing that his friend was unhurt, Tapiola let out a hollow groan. "I think that I have broken a rib," he said, "or possibly a small bone somewhere else."

"Nonsense," said Richard, "don't even imagine such a thing. It is nothing but the shock, and the surprise." To this Tapiola,

after feeling himself all over with his nose, was obliged to agree. "Of course," he said, "if I had seen what was coming, I could have prepared for it, and even given somebody a good bite if necessary; but the trouble is, it always happens to me when I am not looking or do not expect it."

"You must learn to make the best of things," Richard told him, "and to expect the worst. Would you like me to sing for you? I feel that I should like to clear my throat. I could sing you the Shepherd's Lament, if you like."

"No thank you," replied Tapiola, "I do not feel up to it. Not that I am not grateful," he added hastily, "but I am afraid lest someone should hear you, and then we would both of us be sent back home again."

The canary considered this in moody silence. "Well," he said at last, "you may be right, of course, about people hearing me; but if we must be silent all the time, I do not see how we shall ever end up as heroes. What I came along for was to let my voice out in a manly way from time to time."

And he ran up a scale under his breath, ending in a trill.

At once a sparrow popped his head out from the other side of a tin can, and gave him a sarcastic look. "See here," said the sparrow. "Isn't one note enough for you? Do you have to sing a dozen?" And flying over, he gave Richard a sharp peck with his beak.

"Maybe that will teach you not to insult honest people like myself," he remarked.

"Help, help," cried Richard, while Tapiola

cowered in a corner and did his best to burrow
down out of sight in the ashes. When the
sparrow had gone, he came up again, and
looked around him with an air of indignation.
"Where are the police?" he exclaimed.
"What an outrage; no one is safe any more."

"Why didn't you help me?" demanded
Richard. "You could easily have seized the
ruffian in your jaws, and pulled off a wing or
a leg. A fine friend you are, I must say."

And he added, "It was only the thought of
the police that kept me from making more of
a row. I am not afraid of sparrows; but I do
not want to be taken home to my cage in Mrs.
Sweeney's kitchen."

"That is just what I was thinking," said
Tapiola, "and that is why I tried to get out
of sight as fast as I could. Supposing I had

done some injury to that fellow; the entire police force would have been out looking for us. However, when we get a little farther away from home, I will show you that I do not intend to take any nonsense from anyone."

He went on to tell his friend how the other day, on Fifth Avenue, he had gotten the better of the Great Dane Ch. Lance von Habich. "I told him a thing or two," he said, "and he had nothing to say, he shut up like a clam. Then I simply walked away. However, it was

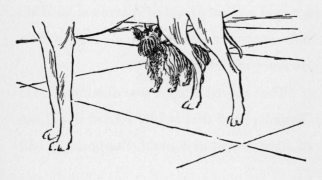

nothing. What I mean to do in future will put everything like that to shame."

So saying, he clicked his teeth with a ferocious sound.

"As a matter of fact," said Richard, "it was the trill that was a mistake. People do not like coloratura any more. When we get out into the country, I am going to practice the Vagabond Song. Then they will know that I am a baritone, and not to be trifled with." And he hummed to himself: *"Sons of toil and danger."*

Boasting in this way of what they intended to do, they passed the time while the truck jolted along in the direction of the river, where a barge was waiting to receive the ashes and tow them out to sea. Thus they found themselves presently dumped once again, in a shower of bottles and tin cans; and this time quite thoroughly buried. When they finally dug themselves up into the light, the barge was bobbing sluggishly along behind a tugboat, and the air was salty with brine. "Well," said Tapiola, sneezing, "I did not expect anything like this to happen to me when I left Mrs. Poppel. Where do you think we are, Richard?"

The canary looked around; but as he was too low to see anything, he flew a little way up into the air to get a better view. When he came down, he looked surprised and disconcerted. "My friend," he said in a grave voice, "we are at sea; we are embarked upon an ocean voyage. At this moment we are passing a large lady holding a candle; she seems to be waiting for someone to come home, just as I have often seen Mrs. Sweeney waiting for Mr. Sweeney."

"She did not look like Mrs. Poppel?" asked Tapiola anxiously.

"I do not think she was anyone we have ever met before," said Richard. "However, since we are apt to be here for quite some time, I think it would be a good plan to explore the ship, and have a look at our fellow passengers, that is if there are any."

The two friends picked their way across the ashes toward the bow. "Let us," said Tapiola, "seek out the dining room first, because this sea air has given me a wonderful appetite."

And with an exclamation of joy, he hurled himself forward in order to seize in his teeth an old bone which he saw a few steps away.

However, before he could reach it, a young
rat ran up and sat down on it. "Yes?" said the
rat, with an unpleasant expression. "You
wanted something?"

"Oh no," said Tapiola hurriedly. "Not at
all.

"Pardon me."

So saying, he turned to leave. Then he saw
that the whole barge was full of rats of all
ages and sizes, hurrying and scurrying, nos-
ing about to see what they could find, and not
hesitating to give each other fearful bites
whenever there was a dispute about anything.
Suddenly an old gray rat stood up on his hind
legs next to Tapiola, and exclaimed,

"Oh rats, my bowels, I am pained at my
very heart. A wonderful and horrible thing
is committed in this land. For from the least

of them even unto the greatest of them,
everyone is given to covetousness. Behold, I
will bring evil upon this people; the neighbor
and his friend shall perish. We looked for
peace, but no good came; and for a time of
health, and behold trouble."

Turning to Tapiola, he said sadly,

"They will not listen to me."

He continued: "Within an hour we shall
all be dumped into the sea and drowned, but
that does not keep them from killing one another for the sake of an old bone or some
other morsel.

"I tell you, we are doomed. The carcasses
of this people shall be meat for the fish of the
sea; and none shall fray them away."

And he added in a voice of despair,

"It will be somewhere off Staten Island."

At these words Tapiola grew pale; and Richard uttered a croak of anguish. "This is your fault, Tapiola," he exclaimed. "It was you who said let us hide in the ash can. You will remember that I wished to fly away at once. Now we are to be drowned; and that is the end of our being heroes.

"Oh my golden cage with its little piece of apple at Mrs. Sweeney's, if ever I see you again I will go inside and stay there."

Tapiola replied gently to the canary,

"You need not drown, or even be dumped into the sea, because you have wings and can fly away. Spread your wings, Richard, and save yourself; and do me the favour to tell Mrs. Poppel that at the last I was brave and resigned. She will find the rubber bone under the sofa. Goodbye, my friend; think of me sometimes, when you are near the water."

And he turned his face away, and closed his eyes.

When he opened them, a few minutes later, Richard was still there. "What," he exclaimed; "haven't you gone yet?"

Richard replied with emotion, "Do you really think I would leave you? What do you take me for? No; we set out to be heroes together; and whatever happens, nothing shall separate us. Besides, there is no hurry, we are not yet off Staten Island, and it is still too far from land for me to attempt it."

Tapiola thanked him with tears in his eyes. "It is much better not to be drowned all alone," he admitted, "or in the company of strangers. Well, since we still have some time left us, let us see if we cannot find a way to escape from this dilemma. What we need is a small boat, or raft; it would be easy, then, to push off by ourselves, and drift with the tide."

"Is that all you want?" asked Richard. "Look behind you."

Tapiola turned, and saw a plank of wood about three feet long, at both ends of which was nailed a small log. "That is just the thing," he said. "Help me to get it over."

He set to work to drag it to the side of the barge, helped by Richard, who fluttered in front of him, and told him where to go. It was hard work, but despair gave him strength, and before long the little raft stood poised like a see-saw above the water. Then Tapiola said,

"I will go out on it; and when my weight

is over the water, it will fall off into the sea."

But as he started to walk out on the piece of wood, the old gray rat ran up to him, and cried,

"Take me with you."

"By no means," said Tapiola; and Richard added,

"No indeed."

The rat did not stop to argue, but pushed his way out along the plank; with the result that in a minute the whole thing fell into the bay with a splash. Tapiola found himself under water; and wild with fear, thrashed about as hard as he could. This brought him to the surface again before he had time to drown, and with such force that he shot half way up onto the raft, on which the old rat and Richard were already seated. "Come, Tapiola,"

said Richard, "get on, and do not thrash
about so or you will have us all in the water
with you."

Tapiola climbed onto the raft, and sat
down. Then he got up and shook himself,
while the others hung on for dear life. After
that he lay down again, feeling very uncom-
fortable. "Couldn't you have waited?" he said
gloomily to the rat.

"Why?" asked the rat. "Waiting never got
me anything."

The raft drifted idly in the tide, the waves
slapped against it gently, and seagulls with
fierce, inquisitive cries flew down to find out
if there was anything to eat. Far off behind
them the city rose out of the sea-mist like a
dream, while ahead in the distance the ill-
fated barge wallowed along toward Staten

Island, bearing its load of doomed and covet-
ous rats. Tapiola shivered, and buried his
nose in his paws; he felt that an ocean life did
not suit him. The wind was cold, and the
water looked dark and dangerous; there was
no place to hide; and he regretted with all his
might having left the comfortable security
of Mrs. Poppel's sofa.

As he lay there under the wide and open
sky, a gull suddenly swooped down and sank
his talons into Tapiola's fur. The attack was
too sudden for the little dog; he let out a
squeak, and at the same time felt himself
being lifted into the air. Richard, deciding
that all was lost, and overcome with horror,
hid his head under his wing; but the old rat
whose aged and yellow teeth could not have
gnawed even a banana, sprang up and with

a ferocious expression fastened his jaws around the gull's leg. With a squawk the big white bird let go its prey, and Tapiola fell back onto the raft with a bump. As soon as he had recovered his breath, he said to the rat,

"You alone have saved my life. While my friend, who is sworn to help me, did nothing, and put his head under his wing, you rushed forward and saved me from death. Thank you; it was a brave deed, and I shall not forget it."

"It was nothing," replied the rat mod-

estly. "Tit for tat. If it had not been for you and your raft, I should be at this moment at the bottom of the sea, along with Pharaoh's hosts, and the inhabitants of Sodom and Gomorrah."

He cleared his throat, made husky by emotion, and continued: "But perhaps I ought to introduce myself; for as we are likely to be companions upon this raft for some time, it will increase our pleasure in each other's company to know who we are." "You are right," said Tapiola, "and I should be only too glad to hear your story, as I fear that we have a long journey ahead of us."

So saying, he settled down to listen to the Story of the Rat.

"My name," said the rat, "is Jeremiah; it is characteristic of the older prophets to live through the disasters they foresaw. My parents dwelt in Saint Margaret's Cathedral, where I myself was born some time ago. Under the circumstances, you will not be surprised to hear that I evinced an interest in the services while I was still no bigger than a mouse, and decided to take orders at an early age. My career started auspiciously; and for a while I was in demand at all the better churches, where my good looks and powerful voice, plus a certain theatrical quality, endeared me to the congregations. However, one day I had a conversion, or rather an illumination. It was while I had been living at Saint Agatha's; and it was there, while I was in the midst of a sermon, that word was brought in that a large piece of cheese had been found under the chancel. At once there

was a rush in that direction, led by myself;
but all of a sudden a voice seemed to say in
my ear, Thou shalt not eat of it, for the day
that thou eatest thereof thou shalt surely die.
I lost no time in repeating these words to the
congregation, who refused to listen to me. I
begged, I pleaded, I even threw myself
beneath their feet, but all to no avail; they
thought me mad, and even went so far as to
say that I wanted the whole cheese for myself. Pushing me aside, they fell upon the
food with cries of joy; and an hour later they
were dead. It was then that I realized that
the spirit of prophecy had entered my breast;
and that I would never be the same again.

"My life since then has not been a happy
one. I can say that my popularity vanished
with my congregation, almost overnight. I

soon found that other congregations which had once delighted to listen to me, shrank from me as from a ferret or a terrier . . . dear me, I beg your pardon."

"Don't mention it," said Tapiola. "Proceed, I beg of you."

"The truth is," said Jeremiah, "I had become known as a croaker. It was said that I no longer told people what they wished to hear; and for that reason my usefulness as a preacher was at an end. The fact that my prophecies invariably turned out as I predicted only served to aggravate the situation. I did my best to limit my sermons to the eternal verities, the decalogue, and the life hereafter, but the spirit of prophecy would not let me alone; I foresaw everything, and everything for the worst. If a congregation

wished to move to new quarters, I knew in advance that they would not find any wood shavings there; if they reveled in an ancient tenement, I knew that it would be torn down. As a result, they began to pull long faces whenever they saw me; I was reduced to preaching in cellars or in the streets where even the sparrows made fun of me; while I watched, with indescribable anguish, my friends and relatives hastening down the road to their destruction. Today I saw the barge tied at the wharf, and jumped on board, thinking to save at least one soul from the fate in store for it. The barge left before I could get to shore again; and I believed that my end had come. The rest you know."

"I am sorry for you," said Tapiola, "because of all things in the world, the most uncongenial is to have to tell people the truth about themselves. That is why," he added with a dark look at Richard, "I do not always say what I think, which is that some people are cowards, even if they can sing like Patti or Lotte Lehmann."

At these words Richard ruffled his feathers, and assumed a truculent air. "Look here," he exclaimed. "I am a baritone."

"And I," replied Tapiola, "am an Irish sheep dog."

"So you are," agreed Richard coldly, "from your manners. It is only too bad that we have no sheep on board."

"Gentlemen," said Jeremiah anxiously.

"If we did," said Tapiola, "they would all be listening to your concert."

"On the contrary," said Richard, "they

would ask you how to fight sparrows."

"Low fellow."

"Nincompoop."

"You are rocking the boat," cried Jeremiah.

The two heroes sat down, while sparks continued to flash from their eyes. "We are at sea," said Jeremiah, "encompassed by the raging elements. This is no time for public quarrels. Put aside your differences, I beg you; submerge them in the common good. Do not be like the tribes of Ephraim and Jephthah, who, at the passage of the Jordan, smote one another hip and thigh over the pronunciation of the word shibboleth. Be rather like David and Jonathan, of whom it is said: And Jonathan caused David to swear again, because he loved him; for he loved him as he loved his own soul."

These words caused Tapiola to feel ashamed of himself. "Very well," he said. "I will do as you wish." And turning toward his friend the canary, he exclaimed, "Richard, accept my forgiveness."

"Accept mine also," said Richard. He added firmly,

"But please remember that I am a baritone."

At that moment the raft grounded upon a sand bar; and looking up, the voyagers saw that they had come to rest on the beach of what appeared to be an island. Giving thanks to heaven for this timely deliverance from the perils of the deep, in which they were led by Jeremiah, they scrambled overboard to shore, and crossing a narrow shelf of sand, discov-

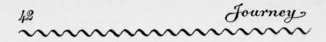

ered a road which led upward toward a village discernible in the distance.

As they proceeded up the road between the trees, Jeremiah remarked,

"Let us give thanks to God, who has brought us out of the land of the Egyptians into a country overflowing with milk and honey."

This remark was the beginning of a discussion on the nature and purposes of God in which all three of the companions joined.

Tapiola said that God was mainly notable for His heroic qualities. "He has been present at all the great battles of history," he declared, "and usually on the winning side. One can imagine Him as being of great size, with flashing teeth, and a tail that sweeps the skies. Otherwise it is hard to account for the constant winds which pour across the earth from every direction. At the same time I imagine Him to be mild and beneficent, and covered with a coat of the softest fur."

"That is out of the question," said Richard. "Since He lives on high, he must obviously have wings; and wings without feathers are by no means practicable. As for a tail, He would certainly need one to ascend and descend; but it does not so much create the breezes, as make use of them. When you speak of His size, who knows? I am inclined to agree with you that He is very large, probably as large as an eagle, but more musical."

The rat joined in to remark that they had both overlooked God's most obvious attribute, which was wisdom. "You say that He is large, and that He flies," he declared, "but

that does not take into account the infinite
subtlety of His creations. Nothing in this
world is arrived at in a direct and straight-
forward manner; even a crumb of bread is the
result of the most intricate relationships.
And so small a thing as a snowflake is in real-
ity a very complicated structure. The God
who created the butterfly out of the cocoon
has by no means a simple and limited intel-
ligence. He is devious and clever; and I think
He uses His tail to balance Himself when
He wishes to sit up on His hind legs.

"As for music, I have no ear myself for
anything but a good squeak."

"I believe," said Richard unkindly, "that
your ancestors were not altogether unmind-
ful of the flute."

"That was in Germany," replied Jeremiah, "and besides, it was a fairy story. Actually what they followed was a wonderfully sweet odor which the piper had sprinkled on his clothes. This has been established by Professor Heinrich von Eckenmeier of the University of Göttingen, and other learned authorities. There has been no odor like it in Germany since. Some scholars believe it to have been the fragrance of love."

"Ah," said Richard, "love." And without being aware of it, he gave utterance to a low trill.

Jeremiah continued: "If one is to accept this explanation, it proves that God took no part in the affair at Hamelin; for by no stretch of the imagination can one conceive of God as the God of love. Nevertheless, I recognize in the massacre of an entire innocent community, traces of His heavenly style. Frankly, I do not know what to think."

"Perhaps," said Tapiola, "he does not like rats."

Jeremiah glanced at him in surprise. "That would hardly be likely," he said, "seeing that He Himself is the Father of all rats."

"Never," cried Richard angrily. "He is a canary.

"A bass canary," he added.

"You are both of you mad," exclaimed Tapiola. "Everybody knows that God is a dog."

Menaced on either side by Tapiola's teeth and Richard's beak, Jeremiah shrugged his shoulders. "What does it matter?" he asked mildly. "As long as we have a name for Him, He can be anything you like. It is only what is nameless that keeps me awake at night."

"Well," said Tapiola, "it is still some time before it gets dark, so let us go on now, for I have a good appetite, and am anxious to get to a house where there is a kitchen or a pantry in which it would be possible to find something good to eat." "That is my idea exactly," agreed Richard, "but I would be satisfied with a stable." "I would like to be able to tell you that you would both of you find what you are looking for," said Jeremiah gloomily, "but the truth is that none of us will find any-

thing at all." "No wonder you are unpopular," cried Tapiola, "if that is the way you
talk." "A prophet is not without honor," replied Jeremiah, "save in his own country."

Conversing in this agreeable fashion, they
drew near the village, where the barking of
a large dog caused Tapiola to hesitate, and
finally take up a position somewhat to the
rear of the others. "Perhaps," he said, "it
would be wiser for us to linger here, and let
Richard go on ahead to look around; he can
fly, and no one will notice him." "Oh indeed,"
said Richard, "so no one will notice me; I
suppose they are accustomed to canaries flying around their heads."

Jeremiah broke in to say that he would be
the one to go ahead; and promised to return
as soon as possible with the lay of the land,

and other information. "I am very good at
that sort of thing," he said, "for the life I
have led has taught me to be quick and quiet.
Sit here under this tree, and I will see what
I can find." "I would like some chopped
liver," said Tapiola, but Jeremiah was already trotting toward the village, sniffing the
air, and looking brisk and hopeful.

The two companions sat down under a
tree, and, as people will, commenced to dis-
cuss the experiences they had been through.
"Do you know what is the worst thing of all?"
remarked Tapiola. "It is to realize that one's
education has been laid out along the wrong
lines, and that all one knows is useless. For
instance, I am very good in a small apartment, I have learned to play with a rubber
ball, not to get stepped on, and to use a little

square of newspaper twice a day. But when the seagull took hold of me, I realized that my education had not taught me what to do in such a case."

To this Richard replied: "The same is true in my own life. There is nothing worse than to show your art, and have it turn out to be unpopular. How was I to know that sparrows have only one note? I have never bothered to listen to them. So when that fellow attacked me, I was speechless with astonishment; otherwise I should have given him something to remember me by."

"Exactly," said Tapiola. "It is surprise which renders us helpless. I can see that to be a hero you must expect to find enemies everywhere; and so after this I intend to be ready for anything." "I also," said Richard, "do not mean to be caught napping; when I sing, it will be under a thorn-bush, by myself." "Good," said Tapiola, "that is an excellent idea.

"But what I want now," he continued in a voice which he tried to make sound casual, "is something to eat. The trouble with me is, being so small, my stomach sticks to my ribs very easily. I am sure I should feel much braver if I had a little dish of raw meat, or even some nice thin gruel, like Mr. Woodhouse."

"Who is he?" asked Richard.

"I do not know," replied Tapiola, "except that he is Emma's father, and some relation to a person called Jane who is a friend of Mr. Poppel, and of the critic Stuart Orrin."

"Well," said Richard, who felt badly be-

cause he did not move in good society like his friend, "this conversation is not getting us anything to eat. For myself, I could easily catch a bug, I think, or perhaps a worm, but after all, we are in this thing together, and so I prefer to wait for Jeremiah to return with a slice of apple, or some seeds." "Ah," said Tapiola with a sigh, "I hope he brings me some chopped liver." "I think it very likely," said Richard, "for he is wonderful at that sort of thing." "Thank you," said Tapiola, "for waiting; I do not think I could bear to see you eat a worm just now."

Jeremiah returned at this point, brushing some crumbs of cheese from his whiskers, and looking very doleful. "My poor friends," he exclaimed, "it is as I thought, there is nothing there at all. I am not a prophet for nothing: the larder is bare."

Tapiola gave a cry of anguish. "What," he shouted, "are we to starve within sight of plenty? Such a thing is unheard of in the world today. Are you sure that you did everything possible?"

"I did my best," replied Jeremiah modestly. "I went everywhere, and saw everything. It is a poor community, and strictly guarded. As a matter of fact, I was several times in danger of my life; and once a large gray cat came dashing at me, and I only escaped by the skin of my teeth."

"Perhaps I should have gone myself," said Tapiola thoughtfully. "I get along very well with cats as a rule. There is something about

me which excites their sympathy." "What,"
exclaimed Jeremiah, "do you wish to live on
pity?" "Well, no," said Tapiola; "that is not
the best thing for a hero, I suppose."

He lay down, with his nose in his paws. The
day was nearly done, it was beginning to
grow dark, and the breeze of evening blew a
cold breath upon him. A bat made a low, un-
certain flight, to see what it was like; a dog
howled sadly in the distance, and soft, rus-
tling things went bump in the bushes. Tapiola closed his eyes; he was cold and hungry,
and he was full of fright at the situation in
which he found himself. He thought of his
little basket at home, with its eiderdown
quilt; he remembered the warm smell from
the kitchen; and he pictured to himself other
attractive places where he had been happy

and comfortable, such as behind the sofa, and in Mrs. Poppel's lap. He remembered how the lamps were lighted at about this time, and how they made everything seem festive and secure. Now I know, he thought, what it means to be alone in the wilderness. What terrors lurk in the darkness all about me; it is alive with horrid sounds; I feel that at any moment I may be rent limb from limb. There is nowhere to hide, there is nothing to get under; if Richard were larger, I could crawl under his wing, but as it is, it is obviously out of the question. One should only try to be a hero during the daytime. What good will it do me to have had only the best intentions, if I am found in little pieces in the morning? Oh my mistress, dear Mrs. P., if only I were back home with you again, I would never stir outside the door. I would always use the little squares of newspaper, and not make any trouble for anybody. Forgive me for leaving you; and send me some generous thought to warm me in this frosty hour; for I know that you will be grieved if I am a corpse by to-morrow, and that is what I will be, I feel sure, far away from those I love.

He also tried to comfort himself by re-membering all the succulent dishes he had eaten in the past, the creamed spinach, the oatmeal and milk, the chopped liver, and even a knuckle bone as big as his head which he had enjoyed all one summer in the country. However, it was in vain; and he presently burst out with: "Oh what would I not give for even one dry biscuit, to sustain the little flame of life which I feel is already so low

within me. Alas, my dear mistress, you will
not even be able to gaze upon these wasted
bones, picked clean by the ravens, because no
one will bother to tell you where they are."

He was silent, shivering to himself; when
suddenly he heard at his side a voice which
in his misery he had forgotten. It was Richard, who exclaimed in trembling tones,

"Tapiola, are you there?"

"My friend," exclaimed Tapiola joyously,
"yes, I am here. I cannot see you, because it
is too dark."

"I know," said Richard, trying to keep his
bill from chattering; "it is not at all the sort
of comfortable obscurity I used to enjoy at
home, under the blanket of my cage at night.
There, at least, there was nothing to see;
while here I am sure there are dreadful things

to see, only I cannot see them."

"It is true," agreed Tapiola. "My poor Richard. But I am glad to know that you are near by."

"Alas," said Richard. After a moment he continued more hopefully,

"Would you like me to sing for you? It is very comforting to have a bit of music now and then, in the midst of troubles."

Tapiola assented eagerly; and clearing his throat, Richard began in a wavering manner the Shepherd's Lament.

"You could not think of something gayer?" asked Tapiola after a while, "or in a less wild and dismal mood? What I would like to hear is something of a tender nature, like Sur le pont D'Avignon, which always reminds me of my childhood."

Richard obligingly changed his tune to
The Bells of St. Mary's; and Tapiola, putting his nose down on his paws, fell quietly
asleep next to Jeremiah, whom neither the
singing nor the conversation which preceded
it had caused to awaken from his slumbers.

Tapiola woke up before the first rays of
the sun had warmed the air, and staggering
to his feet between his sleeping friends, gave
a sneeze which did not, however, disturb
them. He was cramped with cold, and from
being hungry; his stomach stuck, as he had
said, to his ribs; and his legs would scarcely
support him. In this unenviable state, occasionally sitting down as his hindquarters
gave way, but at the same time greatly re-
lieved to find himself still alive after the
night, he made his way up a little hill toward

a house which seemed still, like Richard and
Jeremiah, to be sunk in slumber. The blue
mist of early morning rose from the ground
before him, and surrounded him with a mysterious silence. He alone in the world seemed
awake and alive; and it was without much
hope that he made his way as quietly as possible toward the house whose shuttered win-
dows concealed with indifference the life
within.

What was his joy, then, to discover on the
back steps a dish of milk set out. But it was
not set there for him; for as he approached in
an eager but diffident way, with his tail between his legs, a large white cat rose from
beneath the steps, and exclaimed,

"Well?"

Tapiola stood still. "Excuse me," he said.

And as she continued to eye him with distrust, he added hurriedly,

"I was just out for a stroll. What a lovely morning it is. The climate here is very salubrious."

At that moment his hindquarters gave way again, and he sat down with a bump. The cat looked him over not without sympathy. "You are hungry," she said. "Is that not the truth?"

"Is is," said Tapiola, with a dry swallow.

"You should have said so," remarked the cat, "and not talked all that nonsense about the weather. Here, try this milk; it is watery stuff, but better than nothing."

Tapiola gazed at her in astonishment. "Do you mean me?" he asked. "Are you really offering me your milk?"

"Why not?" she replied. "I am sorry for you. You are so small you make me feel good. And that ribbon in your hair—it is irresistible. You are a dog, aren't you? Well, when I see a dog looking like you do, so small and pitiful, I am glad I am a cat. That is, after all, worth a little milk."

"You are very kind," murmured Tapiola; and advancing to the dish, shyly dipped his nose in.

"If I were your mother," said the cat, "I would not let you out of my sight."

"My mother," said Tapiola, lifting his nose out of the milk, and taking a breath, "is dead. I have been cared for by Mrs. Poppel, the wife of the publisher."

"I know nothing about her," said the cat, "but I am convinced that she is a careless

woman." And she gazed at Tapiola in a melt-
ing and motherly way which caused him to
feel uneasy.

"I hope you will not misunderstand me,"
he said uncomfortably. "I am really quite
sturdy; but you see me under the worst possible conditions. I have actually been all but
drowned in the sea."

"You are such a sweet little dog," said the
cat, and gave him a sudden caress with her
tongue.

"Madame," cried Tapiola, "what are you doing?"

For answer, she rubbed herself against him with a voluptuous purr.

Tapiola was embarrassed; he was even a little frightened. He thought of his glorious career; and his heart sank. What, he thought, am I to let myself be adopted for the sake of a dish of milk? And showing his teeth, he uttered a low growl.

At once the cat gave him a hard slap with her paw, which knocked him head over heels. "Do not growl at me," she exclaimed.

And she added,

"If there is to be any biting in this affair, I will do it myself."

She continued in gentler tones: "Come; I like you, you arouse a feeling of motherliness in me. Be glad that I am of an affectionate nature; and that you are the object of those affections. With me you can live at least as well as with Mrs. Poppel; you can count on milk once or twice a day, and now and then some other tidbit. I will clean your ribbon for you, and you will look very handsome. You will have a great social success."

And she went on to describe the advantages he would enjoy living with her.

Tapiola felt confused. It seemed to him that sirens were singing, and that he was in great danger; he felt himself being carried down into the depths. A feeling of weakness and compliance took hold of him, and he closed his eyes, experiencing a sense of voluptuous joy. But suddenly he remembered his duty; and gave himself a shake. This is the

voice of evil, he thought; this is Circe, at-
tempting to make a swine of me. Oh my
friends, Richard and Jeremiah, do not be
afraid, I will not desert you.

And backing away like a little crab, he suddenly turned, and fled as fast as he could
down the hill the way he had come. The cat
watched him go with regret, but with a shrug
of her shoulders. "Little fool," she said, "go,
then, to your Mrs. Poppel. Probably you
would not have suited me, anyway."

She sat down, and, lifting a leg, gave herself over to the morning bath.

Tapiola arrived soon after at the foot of
the hill among his friends. They were already awake, and ready to depart; and they
stared in surprise at the little dog who burst
in upon them at top speed, with his tongue

hanging out. "Well, well," said Jeremiah, "I
see that something has been chasing you."
And Richard added in a displeased voice,

"Coward."

At the same time, they both got out of
sight as fast as they could, in case whatever
was chasing Tapiola should suddenly appear.

"You are mistaken," said Tapiola, when
he had got his breath back. "I was not pur-
sued and no one attacked me. I did not flee
from an enemy; I fled from love."

"Do not fool yourself," said Jeremiah,
coming out from under a stump where he had
hidden himself, "they are the same thing.
When Salome, the daughter of Herod, saw
John the Baptist for the first time, she felt
an irresistible desire for him. Since he refused
to entertain her proposals, she consoled her-

self with his head, which she caused to be severed from his body, and placed on a silver salver."

These words caused Tapiola to shudder, and to look anxiously behind him. "Let us go away from here," he said.

"By all means," agreed Jeremiah. "But in which direction shall we go?"

"I have not thought about it," said Tapiola. "It makes no difference to me."

"Very well, then," said Richard. "In that case, let us go to Hollywood."

And puffing out the feathers of his breast, he added,

"Whom do I remind you of?"

When his friends confessed that they did not know, his face fell. "Do you not think that I look a little like Mr. Eddy?" he asked.

"I do not know about that," said Jeremiah, "because I have never seen him. But now that you speak of it, I have seen a picture of Mendelssohn, and there is the same beaky look to the two of you."

"Oh," said Richard with disappointment, "Mendelssohn. He was not a great singer; he was not a baritone at all. Have you ever heard me sing the melodies of Victor Herbert?" And without waiting for an answer, he launched himself into the Italian Street Song from Naughty Marietta.

"Tra, la, lalalalala . . ."

"That is not a very manly piece," said Jeremiah. "When I heard it on the stage, it was sung by a woman. However, it suits your voice very well."

"I can also," said Richard, "sing it in a

lower key. Perhaps that would give it more of a baritone effect. Still, after all, if I am going to Hollywood . . .

"Perhaps it would be better if I were a soprano."

"That is entirely up to you," said Jeremiah.

"I will see," said Richard, "when I get there. It is largely a question of salary. Meanwhile, I shall continue to improve my chest tones."

By this time the three companions had left the little grove in which they had spent the night, and, skirting the village, saw before them the open road. Tapiola ran forward a few steps to explore a bush by the wayside; after which he rejoined the others. They then engaged in the following discussion:

"It is hard for me to believe," said Tapiola, "that love and hatred are as closely related as you say. Of course I am not very big, but my heart is large, and I have been in love more than once. I experienced in each instance an emotion of indescribable tenderness, mingled with respect; with occasionally some sadness and loss of appetite. In my opinion love is a sort of medicine, it is a tonic which stimulates certain parts of the body at the expense of others."

"Does not hatred do the same?" asked Jeremiah.

"I am talking about love," said Tapiola.

He continued:

"It seems to me that the objects of my affections aroused in me from time to time a feeling of nobility, with the desire to jump about, and otherwise enjoy myself."

"It is true," said Richard. "Sometimes during the spring I have the same sensations as before a concert, a feeling of worry, with pressure like gas on the heart, fluttering of the breath, nervousness, and at the same time a desire to do something important. Then I am at my best as a singer, and often astonish my friends."

"Love," said Tapiola severely, "is meant to be enjoyed in silence; although music, if low and agreeable, is sometimes a pleasant accompaniment. The influence of the seasons, the shy suggestions of the moon and stars, the warmth of summer and of our natures often combine to bring about a ferment of the senses which I am very partial to."

"You are both of you sentimentalists," exclaimed Jeremiah, "and what you have been describing is not so much love as anxiety. You, Richard, are satisfied with a loud high C; and Tapiola befuddles himself with dreams."

"Pardon me," said Richard; "I reach an F in alt."

"I, on the other hand," continued Jeremiah, "do not confuse love with either worry, or conversion of a religious nature. It is just a business with me. I take it as it was meant to be taken; and it is soon over. It is a pleasure which should be regarded as such; but in addition, it has this practical aspect: it fills the world with rats."

"And did you never," asked Tapiola, "know the tender joy of nestling next to a warm and furry friend, surrounded by blissful odors, and the memory of joy?" "I have no friends," said Jeremiah simply, "and as for odors, there is nothing in the world to compare to a fine ripe cheese."

Tapiola was so offended by this remark that he refused to say anything more. But Richard, to whom one odor was like another, took up the discussion. "The quarrel I have with you, my friend," he said to Jeremiah, "is that you have no pride. You do not understand what it is to excel, to stand out in front of people. What joy, what excitement, to lean as it were upon the air, and create a sound which fills everyone with admiration. That is what love is for, to help the artist. I would not give two cents for a singer who had never known this emotion."

The sun shone warm and pleasant, and the

grass made a fresh odor in the air, sweetened by some flowers of the early season. A butterfly fluttered along before them, and Tapiola gazed at him with the greatest pleasure. Exquisite creature, he thought, how simple life is for you; you have all that is needed to inspire respect and even love; for no one expects you to be anything but beautiful. You do not have to be a hero, and lie out at night on the cold, damp ground.

At the same time, he was obliged to admit that he felt very well after his experiences; the aches of the night before had already vanished from his bones. He trotted along, sniffing the balmy air, and every now and then stopping to look under a stone, to see what there was of interest. All at once he saw Richard dart forward, and seize the butter-

fly in his beak. Then Tapiola remarked sadly
to Jeremiah: "Even beauty is not safe in this
world."

"In the midst of life," said Jeremiah, "we
are in death. Nevertheless, our friend's meal
will not agree with him, because he is not
used to such a diet."

And as a matter of fact, Richard soon com-
plained of pains in his stomach. Tapiola consoled him with the following discourse:

"Richard, my friend, it has been said by the
poet Euripides, and translated by Mr. G.
Murray of Oxford, England,

'The fiercely great
Hath little music on his road,
And falleth when the hand of God
Shall move, most deep and desolate.'

I do not mean to suggest by this that it is God who is responsible for your stomach-ache. No, Richard my friend, it is your own greediness and the violence of your nature. After all, you are an artist, and you ought not to try to swallow a butterfly with one snap of your beak. Have you no respect for beauty unless it is able to sing a scale? I have often heard it said at Mrs. Poppel's that only the writer is by nature generous and forbearing; the painter and the musician think only of themselves. As a result of this—which I now see to be the truth—you have a stomach-ache, and there is one less butterfly in the world. I am ashamed of you; but I think that if you would eat a little grass you would feel better."

Richard hung his head with a very mortified expression; and presently brought the butterfly up again, after which he felt better, and exclaimed:

"It is such experiences as this, in which the artist touches the depths of anguish, which give to art its nobility and breadth."

They continued on their way, enjoying the flowers and the sweet airs of morning, until they came presently to where a large beetle was engaged in dragging himself with gouty difficulty across the path. His enormous jaws stuck out in front of his head; and he had an insolent and ferocious expression. Encased in armor stronger than steel, he expected his angry looks and his hard shell to defend him against attack. He was truly calculated to fill his enemies with terror, just to look at him; but for all that, they soon found out that he was not very intelligent. As Tapiola approached him, he turned in a ponderous manner, and waved his arms. "Go back," he said in a deep voice, "audacious animal. Do not disturb me."

Tapiola was taken aback at this remark, and felt frightened at the angry mien of the beetle, who stood boldly in the way, clicking his great jaws. He wished to retire, and make a detour; but as he stepped back, he trod upon Richard, who had already taken up a comfortable position at the rear. "What," cried Richard, "are you afraid of this old fogey? Never mind, I am behind you. Let us show this apparition from the prehistoric past what sort of people we are. Give him a bite, Tapiola; for I am convinced that he cannot hurt us."

"I do not know about that," said Tapiola

doubtfully. "Did you see his jaws?"

"I do not care two cents about his jaws," said Richard, hopping back a little further. "The question is, are you a hero, or not?"

Encouraged by these words, Tapiola approached the beetle, and licking his lips which had gone a little dry, remarked,

"Sir, I do not intend to allow my path to be disputed by any apparition from the prehistoric past, however formidable."

"Go away," said the beetle. "As for the prehistoric past," he added, "I do not know what you are talking about. I am simply what my ancestors have made me, a tough and rugged individual. As for you, you are obviously something recent, and should be discouraged by all right-minded people."

And he gave his jaws such a ferocious click that he fell over on his nose.

"What I want," he said when he had got up again, "is to go about my business without interference from outside elements. My business happens to be at the other side of this road. Very well; I got here first, so go away and do not bother me."

"The road," said Tapiola with dignity, "is free. My business is at the far end of it. So allow me to pass, if you please."

"The road," replied the beetle heatedly, "is not free. I am on it, so it is occupied. First come, first served; finders is keepers. You are a communist."

"Very well," said Tapiola. "If that is the way you feel about it, then that is the way

you feel about it." And preparing to do
battle to the death, he said farewell to Richard and to Jeremiah. "Goodbye, dear
friends," he exclaimed. "Think of me in the
long winter evenings; remember our adven-
tures together, and in the spring, to keep my
memory green, relate to your children the
story of my life. Tell them that though small,
I was a hero; and that Mrs. Poppel, the wife
of the publisher, wept at my death."

So saying he advanced with a beating heart
upon the beetle, who awaited his approach
with an air of fortitude. When Tapiola had
come to within an inch of his jaws, the beetle
suddenly hurled himself forward and at-
tempted to fasten them in Tapiola's nose.
The little dog let out a cry of terror, and
leaped into the air; and the beetle, pitching

forward with nothing to stop him, fell over onto his back, where he lay helpless with his legs waving in every direction. Tapiola then declared, "I have won a hard battle, with the help of God."

The three companions continued on their way, full of joy and self congratulation; while the beetle, left on his back, was soon discovered by a party of ants, and, still protesting that he did not intend to let himself be interfered with, was taken home by them in

small pieces, where everyone shared alike in the enjoyment of this tough but succulent individual.

"Tapiola," remarked Richard, "there is no question about it, you are a hero."

"Thank you," said Tapiola modestly. "Then perhaps I might go home; what do you think? since I have accomplished what I set out to do."

"Oh," said Richard quickly, "you are not as much of a hero as all that."

He added with a sigh,

"We are still a long way from Hollywood."

And Jeremiah remarked,

"Do not imagine that society will take any notice of your exploit. What is one beetle more or less in the world? In matters of this kind, it is only numbers that count, as it is written: Saul has slain his thousands, and David his tens of thousands."

"And David sang before the Lord," declared Richard with satisfaction. "At least, that is my impression. Correct me if I am wrong."

"You are quite right," said Jeremiah. "But he did not sing any opera. He sang the Psalms, accompanying himself from time to time on the lute."

"I do not care for the lute," said Richard.

Tapiola, who felt that the conversation was getting too far away from his glorious victory over the beetle, took this occasion to remark,

"As a matter of fact, this beetle was a very dangerous fellow. Did you notice how he

jumped at me? And those jaws . . . But I was ready for him; I leaped lightly to one side, and there he was, on his back. That sort of thing is not easy to do, however; it takes courage, let me tell you."

"Well, all right," said Richard. "But just remember who was behind you. Without me, you would be back already where we slept last night."

"That is absurd," declared Tapiola. "I simply recoiled a little before making my leap."

"What is the difference?" said Jeremiah. "The main thing is that we are here, with sound skins, walking along in the fine sunlight. Now we must begin to think about breakfast, because that is what usually comes next at this hour of the day."

Tapiola thought of the milk which he had been obliged to leave behind him on the porch steps, and remarked,

"I could do with a bite of something."

"Very well," said Jeremiah. "Leave it to me. What we need is a plan; we must use our heads a little. Other people have things to eat, so why not we? They must be made to share their delicacies with us, but by cunning rather than by force."

"Yes," said Tapiola. "Still, of course, if you think we should use force . . ."

And he looked around with a fiery but modest air, as though to say Here I am if I am needed.

"The plan I have in mind," said Jeremiah, "is simply this: to make use of what we have. And what have we? We have a singer. You,

Tapiola, have already demonstrated your valor, but as yet Richard has done nothing of moment. What I say is, let him sing; and one of us will pass the hat."

"So I have done nothing," exclaimed Richard indignantly. "And pray what have you done?"

"I have thought up this splendid plan," replied Jeremiah. "In addition, I am willing to be the one to pass the hat."

"What hat?" asked Richard.

But it was impossible for the canary to remain angry very long at a plan which proposed to place him in such a favorable light. "Well, all right," he said at last, "I will sing. I will fill the air with music, in exchange for a piece of apple, or some crumbs of bread. This is after all the destiny of every artist. It is even possible, of course, that someone from Hollywood may hear me; in which case you can take my word for it that by nightfall we shall be able to dine upon the best of everything." "Begin, then," said Jeremiah, "and do not talk so much." "Do you expect me to begin cold?" asked Richard. "I must at least go mimimi a few times to warm my voice." "Very well," said Jeremiah, "warm it if you have to, but do not let us starve to death in the meanwhile." "Have no fear," said Richard, "I will make it up to you in the richest delicacies later on."

And in fact he thereupon poured into the air a fanfaronade of notes, a cascade of trills, scales, arpeggios, runs, and glissandos, pizzicati, and andante, con anima and meno mosso, which in no time at all brought all the birds in the vicinity flocking around him. "What do you think it is?" asked a woodpecker. "I do not know," replied a wren, "for I have never heard anything like it before."

"I do not believe it is real," remarked a catbird; to which a robin replied in doubtful tones, "Still, after all, it has feathers."

"Be careful," said a crow. "You will see—presently it will go off with a bang."

"What—is it a cuckoo clock?"

"It is a mechanical toy."

"It is a sort of whistle."

~~~~~~~~~~~~~~~~~~~~~~~~

At this moment a little red hen came scurrying up with her head held out like a race horse, to see what all the commotion was about. When she saw Richard, she stood still; her mouth fell open, and a look of bliss passed across her face. "I do not care what it is," she exclaimed. "I love it."

And hastily picking up a small bug from the ground, she presented it to the singer in a shy and confused manner.

After this, Richard sang only for the little red hen, who gazed around her with a proud expression. As nothing further was forthcoming in the way of food, Tapiola grew restless, and gave Jeremiah some significant looks. "So," he said in a low voice, "this was your plan, was it? What a splendid idea it is turning out to be. So far, we have received one bug, which Richard ate; but we have had to listen to a great deal of singing."

Jeremiah replied, "Is it my fault if music is not appreciated in this country?"

"We should have taken what we wanted by force," said Tapiola boldly.

"Yes?" said Jeremiah. "From who?"

"Whom," said the little red hen.

With that she added in a breathless voice, "I am a school teacher."

Richard stopped singing; he cut off his song in the middle of a high B flat. "A what?" he asked.

And he gazed at his friends in consternation.

"Then you are not connected with the stage?" he continued. "You are not a successful actress, or even a wealthy enthusiast?"

"Alas, no," replied the hen. "I am only a school teacher. Nevertheless," she added bravely, "you have captured my heart."

"That will be of interest only to my biographers," said Richard. "I will tell them about it."

And with an indignant flirt of his tail, he hopped down from his perch. "Come," he said to his friends, "let us go away from here."

But he did not forget to add, as he disappeared up the road,

"Thanks for the bug."

The little red hen remained rooted to the spot. She felt that her heart was breaking; but at the same time she felt comforted because she was to be put in a biography.

Richard marched up the road in an angry

and flustered manner. He would not have cared if his admirer had turned out to be a writer, or something else of not much importance; but the fact that she was only a schoolmistress mortified him. For he had seen, out of the corner of his eye, some real beauties in the audience, and he was obliged to admit that he had not made an overwhelming hit with them. However, after a while, he began to feel better, and to see things in a happier light; and he comforted himself with the following reflections:

"It is very fine to be an artist, but what is an artist without an audience? And who is in the audience, after all? Simple people, like school teachers and librarians. The singer who cannot win such hearts as these is not worth the trouble of listening to."

To this Tapiola added:

" 'Howe'er it be, it seems to me
'Tis only noble to be good,
Kind hearts are more than coronets,
And simple faith than Norman blood.' "

Richard went on in a thoughtful manner: "I am small, not too plump; and still reasonably young. In addition, I touch the common, every-day heart with my singing. That is something very few people can do; I doubt if anyone has done it in quite such a big way since Jenny Lind. Perhaps it would be a good idea for me to concentrate on Home Sweet Home, instead of To Hell With Burgundy."

"One must consider the spirit of the times," replied Tapiola seriously. "What is

the good of singing Home Sweet Home in
an age when people like to travel around all
the time, and camp out overnight? No,
Richard, art is either of its period, or it is
nothing. That is something I have heard the
critic Stuart Orrin remark. It is true that I
do not admire the singers of today, but then
I have never been popular myself. I am old
fashioned; and to be old fashioned is to be
wrong. It is not for me to advise you, my
friend, for you were born as it were with a
song in your mouth; but I can tell you this,
that if people prefer To Hell With Burgundy, you will only embarrass them by singing Home Sweet Home."

"That is true," said Richard. "Thank you,
Tapiola, for reminding me of what I already
knew. It would be a mistake for me to try to

imitate the great songbirds of the past, when the popular taste runs to something altogether different—something at once more common and more careless, like the times we live in."

"Yes, yes," said Jeremiah, "but all this is not getting us anything to eat."

He glanced gloomily at his companions; then suddenly sitting down on his haunches, he wrapped his paws around his nose. "I have it," he exclaimed; "dunce that I am, why did I not think of it before?"

He continued: "I was mistaken when I imagined that people would pay to hear Richard sing. I should have known that what they really enjoy is a lecture on some cultural topic, such as literature, or travel. Thus they get an education while being entertained; and

later have something to say to each other
across the breakfast table." "Do not talk
about the breakfast table," said Tapiola with
a groan. "Well then," continued Jeremiah,
"Why should we not provide them with an
entertainment of this sort, since in the person
of Tapiola we have both a traveller and a literary genius. At least, he has lived in literary
circles; and while that does not necessarily
make him a genius, still it gives him something to talk about."

"I have never given a lecture in my life,"
said Tapiola. "I would not know how to begin."

"You begin with 'ladies and gentlemen,' "
replied Jeremiah, "and after that you wait
and see."

"What he means is," said Richard, "that

after that you sit down again. I should like to hear Tapiola make a speech . . . well, that's a good one, I must say. What a foul idea."

"Is that so?" said Tapiola, "I have an idea that at least they would know what I was doing; and not take me for a cuckoo clock."

"That is what you think," replied Richard gloomily, "but the truth is, you never know what you are being taken for until after it is too late."

While this spirited discussion was taking place between the two friends, Jeremiah excused himself and went off into the fields with the look of a businessman or a manager. Tapiola and Richard sat down to wait his return, and, lulled by the sun, soon closed their eyes and fell into a light slumber. When they awoke, Jeremiah had come back again; he

seemed to be pleased, and at the same time to be in a hurry. "Come," he said; "I have found what we are looking for. There are a number of serious-minded rabbits in a field near by; and I have convinced them that they would like to hear Tapiola deliver a lecture entitled Literary Afternoons, or Life at Mrs. Poppel's."

And as Tapiola hesitated, he added, "You have nothing to fear, because they have never read a book in their lives."

He concluded in a tone of desperation, "It is our only hope of getting anything to eat; so do not stand there making trouble, but come along for God's sake and do the best you can."

So Tapiola presently found himself in a small garden, among some lettuces, and in the midst of a little group of rabbits, who stared at him, hopped about, waved their ears, and gave each other dubious looks. His throat felt dry, his legs trembled, and he could not think of anything to say. "Go on," hissed Richard, like Beckmesser in Die Meistersinger, "commence."

However, at that moment a plump lady rabbit stepped forward, and with a winsome expression, exclaimed,

"We are fortunate in having with us today a famous figure in the great world of letters. I am happy to introduce to you Mr. Tapiola, who will now tell us something about life at Mrs. Poppel's."

"Who is Mrs. Poppel?" demanded a young rabbit with his mouth full of lettuce.

"Hush," said the lady rabbit; and sat down.

Tapiola took a deep breath. "Ladies and gentlemen," he began in a quavering voice, "I am very happy to be here, in your beautiful lettuce garden. And speaking of lettuces, reminds me of a story . . ."

But he could not remember anything more about the story.

"On the other hand," he said, "I am sure that you would prefer to hear about some of our great writers, like Stuart Orrin, and Robert Nathan. Well, as a matter of fact, I have often seen them, from my place under the sofa; I have been as close to them as I am to you. I can say to you that Mr. Orrin has very big feet. And once Mrs. Poppel said in my presence, 'It is impossible to have a popular success under a thousand pages . . .'

You can imagine that it is very interesting to me to be in the midst of things like that. Mr. Nathan is also an interesting person. Once he said to Mrs. Poppel, 'Mrs. Poppel, I would like to have some more advertising for my books.' He has slightly bowed legs, and a stomach which becomes more noticeable from time to time. He does not wear such fancy shirts as Mr. Poppel."

And he looked anxiously at Jeremiah, as though to ask, How am I doing?

"Who is Robert Nathan?" demanded the young rabbit.

And an elderly rabbit exclaimed,

"Don't you know any good writers?"

Tapiola hurried on,

"Then there is my little bone made of rub-

ber, and my basket with its eiderdown quilt. Yes, everything is very interesting at Mrs. Poppel's."

"Oh boy," said Richard, who had found a small, tasty bug hiding under a lettuce leaf.

Tapiola looked around him at his audience. Several of his listeners seemed to be asleep; out of the corner of his eye he saw a young rabbit hop quietly behind a mound of earth, and then scuttle away down a furrow out of sight. It occurred to him that he was not making a great success as a lecturer; and his tail drooped.

But as he stood there, feeling sorry for himself, and wondering whether to go on or not, his eyes suddenly encountered the soft gaze of a young lady rabbit. She was looking at him with such respect and at the same time with so much admiration, that his heart leaped up into his throat, and a mist passed before his eyes. When it cleared, he ventured to smile at her; and he was enchanted to see that she returned the smile, though in a shy and modest manner.

"Well," said Tapiola bravely, "I shall continue."

He had no sooner uttered these words than a frightful thing happened. With loud barks, a pair of shaggy black terriers came dashing into the garden, and fell upon the rabbits, who fled on all sides with squeals of terror, leaving Tapiola alone to face the enemy. But not altogether alone; for in a single bound the young lady rabbit was beside him, trembling in every limb. "Save me," she murmured. And she added,

"For I know that you are a hero."

Faced with the flashing teeth and gleaming eyes of the oncoming foe Tapiola's heart died within him. The idea of being a hero no longer appealed to him. And turning tail, he fled with a yelp, as fast as he could go, out of the garden and down the road, where his friends Richard and Jeremiah were also making as good time as possible.

The two terriers dashed after him, paying no further attention to the young rabbit, who all but fainted with relief at finding herself overlooked in this way. Ah, she thought, he has drawn them away, he will first wear them out with running, and then turn and demolish them. She believed that he did this for her sake. But Tapiola had no intention of turning, except to remonstrate with his pursuers, whose teeth were already nipping at his hind-quarters. "Look here," he cried over his shoulder, "I am not a rabbit. I am a dog. You could see for yourselves, if you would only stand still for a moment." "Nonsense," replied the larger of the two terriers, "you are a rabbit; don't try to tell us anything else. Don't you think we know the difference? A dog? You? Oh no." And his teeth clicked within an inch of Tapiola's tail.

"Well, then," cried Tapiola in despair, "what have you got against rabbits?"

"Several things," replied the terrier, galloping along behind him. "In the first place, they annoy me because they are so meek. In the second place, they are too bold; they have

too good a time. And finally, if I did not have rabbits to dislike, whom would I have to dislike?"

After a while the terriers grew tired of the chase. Tapiola did not stop running, however; with pounding heart, and his rump smarting from several sharp nips, he tore along until he had caught up to his friends, whom he found at last seated beneath a tree, waiting for him. They sat there because they had come to the end of the road.

Yes, the road stopped there. Before them lay the river; and beyond the river rose a miraculous city, towering into the clouds.

"Well," said Richard, when Tapiola arrived, miserable and out of breath, "where have you been?"

Tapiola did not reply at once; he lay down

and began to lick his wounds. "Where was I?" he said at length. "I was in the thick of battle, where a fighter belongs. But you, you coward . . . I saw your tail disappearing over the horizon, a little ahead of Jeremiah."

"That is right," said Richard simply. "I decided to save myself for my next concert. "However," he added, "let us forget the past; and look instead to the future. See there, across the water . . . what do you see?"

"I see a city," replied Tapiola.

"Yes," said Richard, "but what city? That is the question." "I have no idea," replied Tapiola. "Then I will tell you," said Richard.

And he added in hushed tones,

"It is Hollywood."

"Is it indeed?" said Tapiola. "That is

strange; because it looks familiar, though I have never seen Hollywood before. However, if it is Hollywood, let us waste no time in getting over there, so that Richard can begin his career, and get us something to eat. I see a ferry coming; let us go down to meet it, and engage passage into the future."

"Let us do so," said Richard, "for I am in a hurry to begin."

The three companions descended to the ferry, where they had no difficulty in climbing aboard when no one was looking. Then they made their way to the bow, and looked across the water to the streets and buildings which awaited them. And each one mused upon life, full as it was to him of hopes and disappointments. Only Jeremiah expected nothing very good to come to him in Hollywood; but at the same time he knew that whatever came to him, he would make the best possible use of it. As for Richard, he looked forward to a great success. Yes, he thought, I shall knock them dead. But he did not know whether it would be as a soprano or a baritone. He realized that the successful singer thinks twice about that sort of thing; and that the music is not as important as the composer supposes. What is important, is to make a good effect—either of manly power, if the voice is low, or of charm, if it is high.

We will see which one pays more, he said to himself, when I get there.

Tapiola would have liked to sit down, but his rump was still sore from being bitten. He thought of his battles, of how he had defeated the beetle, and how he had fled from everyone else. It is no use, he said to himself; why do I not be honest with myself? I am no Ch. Lance von Habich; and little dogs like me will never gain popularity through my efforts. Dear Mrs. Poppel, you alone loved and understood me; and I should have been satisfied with that.

But even as he spoke, he remembered how the young rabbit had looked at him, and how she had asked him to save her. And at this, a feeling of joy and peace entered his heart which was still beating so fast from the chase.

I do not know your name, he said to her in his mind, but I shall never forget you. For you alone, of all the people I have known, called me a hero. Perhaps one such person in this life, is enough; for it is true that even Napoleon and Mussolini had people who did not consider them heroes. Whether one is admired by a million, or by only one, there will always be others to whom one is nothing but a Yorkshire terrier.

At the same time he experienced a feeling of sadness, for it came over him that he had left his true love behind him, in the lettuce patch. How she looked at me, he thought, so soft and amiable, with such a tender expression. Yes, she understood me, just like Mrs. Poppel; I could see that. Alas, my dear friend, I do not know what the future holds

for me, but never fear, I shall find you again, for one does not lose an acquaintance such as yours without a struggle.

And he sighed; for he realized that he was lonely. After all, he thought, what does my life amount to? No glory can make up for being alone; and it will take more than a rubber ball to distract my attention from this fact, now that I know it. Yes—what I really want is a quiet domestic life, under the sofa, with the little rabbit at my side. During the day we could play together; and at night fall asleep side by side in my wicker basket, under the eiderdown quilt. With such a little rabbit next to me, I would always be warm and happy.

And because he was not going home, but

was on his way to Hollywood and a glorious career as a hero, a tear ran from his eye and fell to the deck of the ferry boat, on whose deckhouse was to be seen a sign which said "Twenty Third Street."

But all at once he felt a soft nudge at his behind. His mouth at once grew dry; he swallowed with difficulty; and he closed his eyes in anguish. Was it possible that the dreadful terriers were still upon his track? Had they followed him? smelt him out? found him?

And in dying tones he murmured piteously, "I am a dog, not a rabbit."

"Naturally," said a soft female voice. "You do not need to tell me that. But I do not mind."

Opening his eyes with a startled jump,

Tapiola turned to face the little lady rabbit, who stood before him with a demure expression, and downcast eyes. She was not alone, for beside her, on one foot, stood the little red hen, gazing anxiously at Richard.

"I could not let you go," said the rabbit simply. "So I came to share with you the perils and the rewards of your glorious life."

So saying, she looked up at him with a beseeching expression.

"I too," said the hen, "prefer to live with a great artist, even though unwed, than waste away, however morally, in a barnyard."

"The devil," said Richard; and gave a low whistle. "What a situation." However, it could be seen that he was not displeased.

As for Tapiola, his joy knew no bounds. He put his nose close to the rabbit, and gave

her several languishing looks. Then he sat
down beside her, not without a cry of pain,
however; and together, with peaceful and
happy expressions, they watched the approach of the city, in which his fortune was
to be made. They felt no need to say anything; their hearts beat with happiness, with
peace, and with understanding.

The ferry came gently into the dock; and
they walked off into the arms of Detective
Sergeant Murphy, who had been assigned to
the waterfront to look for Mrs. Poppel's
little dog. An hour later they were home, in
Mrs. Poppel's apartment.

She did not try to separate the lovers; since
she was not a publisher's wife for nothing.
Besides, she believed that the little rabbit's
influence on Tapiola would be a good one.

"There is a new look in his eye," she told her husband, who did not like the idea of a rabbit hopping around in his bedroom; "he stands up straight, and holds his tail out; and look how fiercely he plays with his little ball. No, Alfred, let him keep the rabbit if he wants to. Only he must have a bath at once; and a new ribbon for his hair."

Picking Tapiola up in her arms, she embraced him on top of his head, not forgetting to pat the rabbit also, as she put him down again.

That night, in his wicker basket under the eiderdown quilt, Tapiola lay beside his friend, whose fur was soft, and smelt of gardens. His eyes were closed; and his tiny breast, no bigger than that of a squab, expanded in a de-

licious sigh, like a balloon. "Love," he murmured sleepily, "is meant to be enjoyed in
silence."

"Lean thou beside my cheek," quoted the
little rabbit, "and do not speak. Love is not
all; but let no other word Than love be
heard, For as we older grow, Wide wanders
wisdom, but the heart beats slow."

"She is literary, besides," thought Tapiola;
and his cup of happiness overflowed.

Below, in Mrs. Sweeney's kitchen, Richard
and the little red hen sat together in the cage,
under the blanket. "This is cosy, after all,"
he said drowsily, closing his eyes. "And to-
morrow I will begin to practise my chest
tones."

But outside, in the streets, among the

sounds of traffic, of footsteps and wheels, the
murmur of the city which soothed and comforted Tapiola in his wicker basket, Jeremiah
went slowly and alone in search of a congregation. He did not expect to find one; but he
went on, nevertheless, in case anything else
turned up. As he limped along in the gutters,
he murmured: "I was a father to the poor:
and the cause which I knew not, I searched
out. Then I said, I shall die in my nest. Terrors are turned upon me, they pursue my soul
as the wind. Upon my right hand rise the
youth; they push away my feet. They mar my
path. My bones are pierced in me in the night
season; and my sinews take no rest. I am a
brother to dragons, and a companion to
owls."

All at once he chuckled. "I would hardly

call Tapiola a dragon," he said, "or Richard
an owl. Still . . ."

And passing at that moment an old tenement in which a light was still burning, he
called out in a loud voice,

"Any old clothes? Bottles?"

The End

This book is composed in Linotype "Scotch."
This style of type came into fashion in England
and the United States by way of fonts cast at
the foundry of Alex. Wilson & Son at Glasgow
in 1833. It was a style of letter that echoed the
"classical" taste of the time, and would seem to
have been inspired by the kind of letter-shapes
that result when you cut lettering on a copper
plate with a graver—just as visiting-cards are
cut now. It is more precise and *vertical* in char-
acter than the "old style" types (such as Cas-
lon) that it displaced.

———

*This book was designed by Georg Salter. It was
composed, printed and bound by H. Wolff, New
York. The paper was made by Curtis & Brother,
Newark, Del.*

RICHARD

TAPIOLA

Journey of Tapiola

JEREMIAH

J E R S E Y   C I T Y

B A Y O N N E

Here the lecture was held

Here Richard sang

Here was the great beetle

Home of the